P9-BZF-611

Little Epistles for Kids

Barney Wigglesworth and the Church Flood

A BOOK ABOUT HOSPITALITY

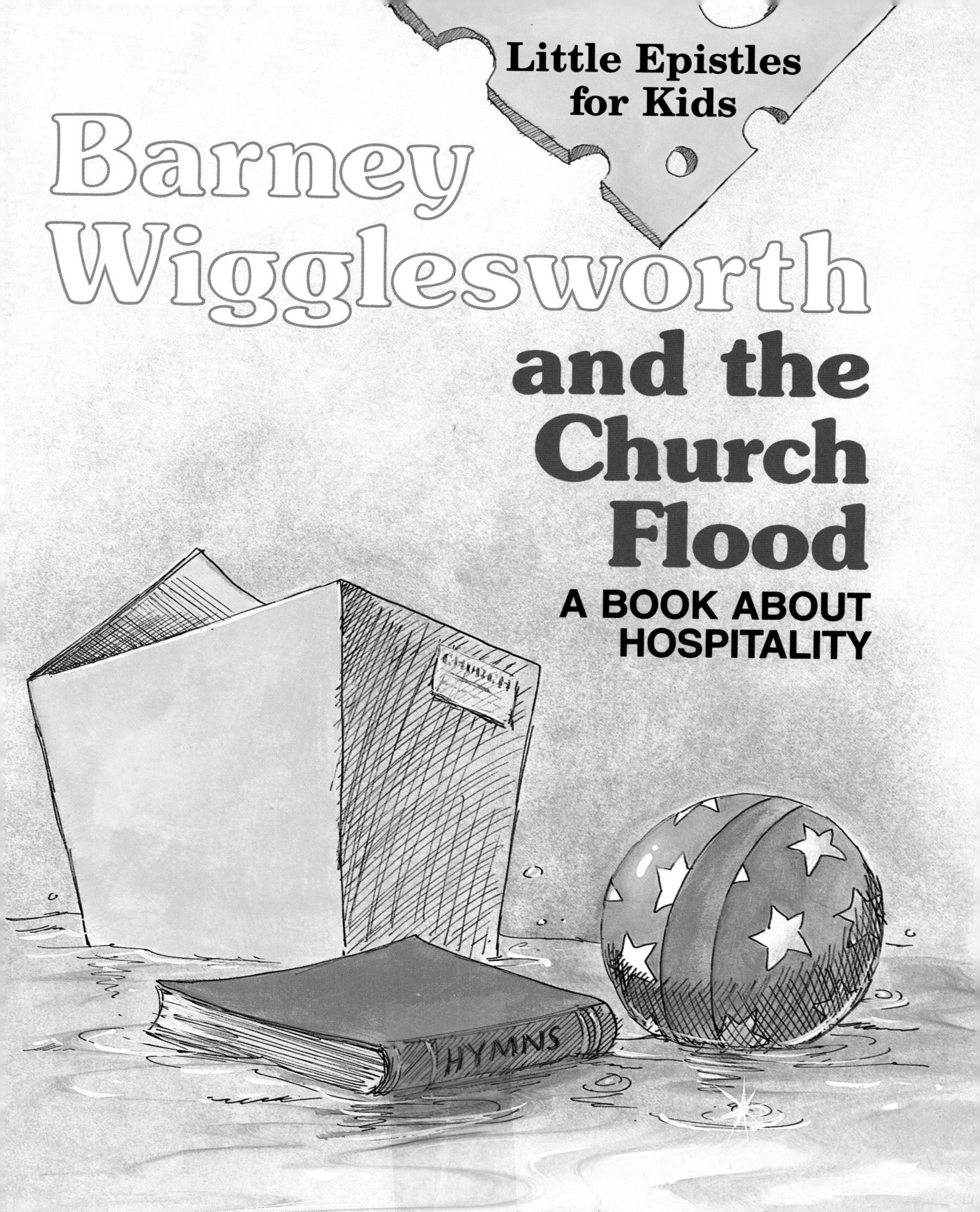

Elspeth Campbell Murphy
Illustrated by Yakovetic

Chariot Books
David C. Cook Publishing Co.

Share with God's people who are in need. Practice hospitality. (Romans 12:13, NIV)

Offer hospitality to one another without grumbling. (I Peter 4:9, NIV)

DEAR PARENTS AND TEACHERS,

Barney Wigglesworth and the Church Flood is a story illustration of hospitality in action. But, as Barney finds out, it's sometimes hard to share and even harder to be cheerful about it.

Young children are rather erratic hosts. They can astound us with sudden bursts of sympathy and generosity. But at other times they cling to their toys and other possessions for dear life. It's as if they think that by sharing something that belongs to them, they're giving away a little bit of themselves. Actually, they're right. Because by learning to share the tangible things (home, food, clothes, toys), they're also learning to give the intangibles from deep within themselves—comfort, for example, and hope.

Of course, such a concern for other people's well-being doesn't spring up overnight. It's an attitude that needs time to grow in children as they—like Barney—see cheerful hospitality practiced by the adults around them.

But why mice? It has been said that animal characters are really "kids in fur coats." Children will readily identify with Barney. But because animal characters are one step removed from real life, the concepts of the book come across in a fun, nonlecturing, nonthreatening way.

(Note: In the book Barney encounters the expression "My house is your house." Ask your children to explain in their own words what they think the statement means.)

Now sit back with your kids and enjoy Barney's adventures.

Chariot Books is an imprint of David C. Cook Publishing Co.
David C. Cook Publishing Co., Elgin, Illinois 60120; David C. Cook Publishing Co., Weston, Ontario

BARNEY WIGGLESWORTH AND THE CHURCH FLOOD

Cover design by Dawn Lauck

First Printing, 1988 Printed in Singapore
93 92 91 90 5 4 3 2

Library of Congress Cataloging-in-Publication Data
Murphy, Elspeth Campbell.
Barney Wigglesworth and the church flood. (Little epistles for kids)
Summary: When Barney the mouse's family takes in a family of flood victims, Barney resents having to play and share his toys with little Christopher.
[1. Hospitality—Fiction. 2. Mice—Fiction. 3. Christian life—Fiction] I. Yakovetic, Joe, ill. II. Title. III. Series.
PZ7.M95316Barn 1988 [E] 88-5008
ISBN 1-55513-685-0

Rain, rain, rain, rain, rain! I wonder if it's ever going to stop! It rained all last night. It rained so much that this morning the church basement was all flooded.

You're probably thinking, "So what's the problem, Barney Wigglesworth? You live in the church balcony. The balcony is too high up to get flooded."

That's true. But there are some mouse families who live in the basement, and the other mice had to rescue them from the flood.

My father brought the Twitchet family home to stay with us until their mouse hole dries out.

"Our house is your house!" he said.

And *that's* the problem.

My mother and father don't think it's a problem. They get to look after Mr. and Mrs. Twitchet.

My sister, Bella, doesn't think it's a problem. She gets to look after Claire Twitchet.

But who do I get to look after? Little old Christopher Twitchet, that's who.

Christopher is a nuisance, pure and simple.

He needed some dry clothes to wear. So my mother said, “No problem! He can have something of Barney’s. I’ll just cut it down to size.”

My shirt! *Snip, snip, snip, snip, snip*. My shirt on little old Christopher Twitchet.

Then for lunch we had macaroni and cheese. (My favorite.) And Christopher asked my sister if he could have the part on top that's almost burnt, because it's crunchy-chewy. (My particular favorite.) And Bella said, "Sure thing, Christopher!"

And *scrape, scrape, scrape, scrape, scrape.* All the crunchy-chewy, almost-burnt parts went onto Christopher's plate.

Then after lunch, I went out to swing on my trapeze. But my father came running after me. “Get down from there, Barney!” he said. “You can’t climb on the chandelier while Christopher is visiting. If he sees you up there, he’ll want to climb, too. But you know he’s too little!”

I took the little nuisance back to my room. "That does it!" I said to Christopher. "I'm going for a walk."

"Can I come, too?" asked Christopher.

"No, you cannot," I said. "You stay here. But don't you dare touch any of my toys!"

So off I went.

And here I am.

Uh-oh. Here comes my sister, Bella, and Claire. They can't see me up here. But I can hear what they're saying.

"Poor, little Christopher," says Claire. "He hated having to leave his toys behind at home."

"Don't worry," says Bella. "He can play with Barney's toys. Barney doesn't mind sharing."

"Where *is* Christopher by the way?" says Claire. "He wasn't anywhere in the house."

"Don't worry," says Bella. "I'm sure he's with Barney. Barney doesn't mind looking after him."

I know what you're thinking. You're thinking, "You are in big trouble, Barney Wigglesworth! You have been a selfish and irresponsible mouse. In short, you have behaved like a rat. You'd better go find Christopher right this minute!"

You're right, of course. I have to go find Christopher. And I have a sinking feeling that I know where he went. I wouldn't let Christopher play with my toys. So . . . what if he tried to go back home to get his *own* toys?

“Christopher! Are you crazy? What are you doing down there?”

“Barney! Help! Help!”

HYMNS

HYMNS

"Christopher, you little squeaker! Promise me you won't *ever* try that again! You know you can't go home until your mouse hole dries out! I'm sorry I said you couldn't play with my toys. Of course, you can play with them. My house is your house. OK, Christopher?"

"OK, Barney."

I know what you're thinking. You're thinking, "Good for you, Barney Wigglesworth! No one ever said sharing is easy, but you are being a very generous and responsible mouse."

Well, thank you for saying so. But the way I look at it—as long as Christopher needs me, my house is his house.

THE END